INVISIBLE

W9-BSQ-106

Volume 1
Mysteries 1-4

by **Elizabeth Levy**

Illustrated by **Denise Brunkus**

Scholastic Reader — Level 4

SCHOLASTIC INC. Cartwheel B·O·O·K·S ®

New York Toronto London Auckland Sydney
Mexico City New Delhi Hong Kong Buenos Aires

To all the children, visible and invisible,
I've met on my travels
—E.L.

For Trinka H. Noble
and all the mysteries of life
—D.B.

No part of this publication may be reproduced, or stored in a retrieval system, or transmitted in any form or by any means, electronic, mechanical, photocopying, recording, or otherwise, without written permission of the publisher. For information regarding permission, write to Scholastic Inc., Attention: Permissions Department, 557 Broadway, New York, NY 10012.

Invisible Inc. #1: The Schoolyard Mystery (0-590-47483-9)
Text copyright © 1994 by Elizabeth Levy.
Illustrations copyright © 1994 by Denise Brunkus.

Invisible Inc. #2: The Mystery of the Missing Dog (0-590-47484-7)
Text copyright © 1995 by Elizabeth Levy.
Illustrations copyright © 1995 by Denise Brunkus.

Invisible Inc. #3: The Snack Attack Mystery (0-590-60289-6)
Text copyright © 1995 by Elizabeth Levy.
Illustrations copyright © 1995 by Denise Brunkus.

Invisible Inc. #4: The Creepy Computer Mystery (0-590-60322-1)
Text copyright © 1996 by Elizabeth Levy.
Illustrations copyright © 1996 by Denise Brunkus.

All rights reserved. Published by Scholastic Inc.
SCHOLASTIC, SCHOLASTIC READER, CARTWHEEL BOOKS, and associated logos are trademarks and/or registered trademarks of Scholastic Inc.

12 11 10 9 8 7 6 5 4 3 2 1   4 5 6 7 8 9/0
Printed in Singapore   10
This edition created exclusively for Barnes & Noble, Inc.
2004 Barnes & Noble Books
ISBN 0-7607-5609-0
First Scholastic printing, May 2004

INVISIBLE INC.

The Schoolyard Mystery

by **Elizabeth Levy**

Illustrated by **Denise Brunkus**

CHAPTER ONE

Tears in the Classroom

Chip Stone walked into his classroom. Bandages covered his face and hands. He looked as if he had been in a giant fire. The whole class gasped, even Keith Broder. Keith was almost never nice to anybody.

Justin's mouth dropped open. Chip was his best friend. He had heard about Chip's accident. Chip looked awful! Chip sat down next to Justin.

Justin scribbled a note that he passed to Chip.

Hey, man, good to have you back!

Chip turned his face to Justin. Justin looked through the bandages but couldn't see Chip's eyes.

He thought he saw a little tear in one corner.

Justin rubbed a tear from his own eye. He sniffled. This pile of bandages was his best friend. Justin would do whatever he could to help Chip get better.

Chip took a pen in his bandaged hand. He could barely hold it. Chip slowly formed each letter. He passed a note to Justin.

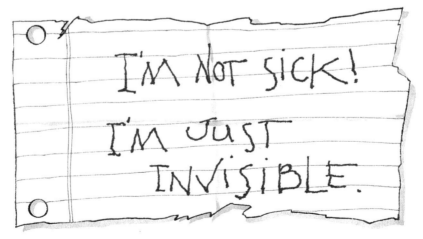

Justin read the note. He wondered if the problem was in Chip's
head. Even if it was, he would still
stick by his friend.

No matter what.

During recess, the teacher,
Mr. Gonshak, brought out a giant
rubber ball. It had all the continents
and seas on it. It was almost as tall
as Mr. Gonshak, and he was six feet.

"The PTO bought this new ball just for the second grade," said Mr. Gonshak. "Isn't it fun? Be careful that Latin America doesn't roll right over you."

The kids shrieked as the ball rolled toward them like a giant bulldozer. Mr. Gonshak went to the swings to talk to Ms. Gerber, the kindergarten teacher.

Keith grabbed the ball and tried
to lift it over his head. It was so big
that he staggered backward and fell.

The ball bounced off his head.
Charlene rolled it away from him.

Keith gave her a dirty look.
Charlene then bounced the ball
toward Justin. It bounced off him. It
was much lighter than it looked.

Justin kicked the ball back to the middle of the group. Chip was standing a little outside of the circle. Justin felt bad. Chip was so heavily bandaged he couldn't play.

Justin walked over to Chip to try

to cheer him up. "Mr. Gonshak is asking Ms. Gerber for a date," Justin said to Chip. Chip giggled through his bandages. He knew all about the times that Justin heard secrets the teachers told each other. Justin couldn't hear well in one ear. His teachers spoke into a special microphone that broadcast straight into a tiny radio Justin wore around his neck. But Mr. Gonshak often forgot to turn the microphone off. Justin heard all kinds of things that he wasn't supposed to. Also, people sometimes forgot that he could read lips.

Then suddenly, Chip walked away like a mummy in his bandages. Justin decided Chip might be lonely.

Justin followed him. Chip turned
a corner by the swings. Then Justin
saw Chip's clothes and a pile of bandages lying on the ground. Had Chip
gone nuts and torn his bandages
off?

"Chip! Chip!" shouted Justin.

Justin felt something clamp over
his mouth but nothing was there!

Justin tried to scream.

"It's me! Chip!" a voice said into Justin's good ear. Justin took a deep breath. The clamp over his mouth felt like a hand. It smelled like Chip. It was warm and human feeling. But Justin couldn't see it!

"Promise not to scream," said the voice.

Justin nodded. Justin felt fingers slowly leaving his mouth. He twirled around to face Chip. But there *was* no Chip! There was just air.

Justin waved his arms in the air. He put his finger out and hit something soft.

"You poked my belly," said Chip.

"Chip?" asked Justin, his voice shaking.

"It's me," said Chip. "In the flesh."

"What flesh?" Justin asked. "I can't see you."

"I know," said Chip. His voice sounded sad. "You can't read my lips. I don't have any lips, but you can hear me, right? I'm talking right into your good ear, okay?"

"I can hear you fine. But what happened to you? Why can't I see you? You can tell me. I'm your friend." Justin reached out to put his arm around Chip's shoulder, but all he got was air. "How did it happen?"

"You know how my mom and dad love to explore caves," said Chip. "We were walking through a cave, and it was dark and a little wet. My foot slipped on some water, and I fell into a pool. I felt cold and wet when I got out, but otherwise I felt fine. It was too dark to see anything in the cave. Then when we came out into the light, Mom was yelling, 'I can hear you, but I can't see you.' She was wailing. I was scared stiff."

"You mean, you didn't break any bones?" said Justin.

"Not a scratch."

Justin stared into the space next to him, trying to figure out where Chip was standing. "This is too weird."

"Weird? *You* think it's weird? Just imagine being *me*. I *feel* fine. But nobody can see me."

"It's easier to see you with the bandages."

"I hate those bandages," said Chip. "The doctor said I should wear them so that kids would treat me normally, but they itch — and nobody treats me normally."

"I'll try," said Justin.

Suddenly, Justin saw something move by the corner of the swings.

"Hey, Justin! Are you reading your own lips? Who are you talking to, dip-lips?" yelled Keith.

Justin rolled his eyes. Keith had such a big mouth, it was easy to read his lips. "Mind your own bees-wax, Keith!" he shouted.

Keith jumped as if he were being

tickled by an invisible hand. He was.

Keith looked at the air next to him. He ran back toward the other kids.

"This could be fun," Chip said just as Mr. Gonshak blew the whistle.

Recess was over. Chip put his bandages back on.

"I'm too old for this," said Justin.

"Old for what?" asked Chip.

"Having an invisible best friend."

CHAPTER TWO
Good Not Evil

"Mom, I'm not wearing the bandages to school," Chip announced when he got home. "It's too hard to talk."

His mother looked worried. "The doctors said that the children in your school may not be ready to accept you as, well . . . different."

"I told Justin what happened to me, and *he* didn't freak," Chip insisted.

The next day Chip put on his clothes and baseball cap — but no bandages.

During show-and-tell, he told the class the truth about what happened.

Charlene raised her hand. "I

think you're very brave," she said.

"Charlene, all I did was trip into a
pool of water in a cave."

"No, I mean to go without your bandages," said Charlene. "To show us who you are."

"He's nothing," said Keith. "He's not even there."

"He is too!" said Justin. "Chip is still the best kid in the class. Three cheers for Chip."

"Hip! Hip! Hooray!" Charlene led the cheering.

The air around Chip's baseball cap turned a slight shade of pink.

"Now that's enough of that," said Mr. Gonshak. "Just because Chip is invisible doesn't mean we may call out in class. Rules are rules."

Then Mr. Gonshak turned toward Mary. "Now, Mary, remember your promise to bring in something for show-and-tell tomorrow."

Mary wouldn't look up. She was very shy. She hardly ever talked in class.

The next day, Mary walked to the front of the room, holding a little cage very tightly. "This is my salamander," she whispered. "His name is Doormat because I found him on my doormat."

"Do you want to tell us anything else about him?" asked Mr. Gonshak.

Mary shook her head.

"If you stepped on him, he'd be dead as a doormat," said Keith.

"That's a dormouse, dingbat," said Charlene.

"You mean dead as a doornail," said Justin.

Mary looked horrified. She didn't like the talk about dead salamanders. She held Doormat's cage even tighter.

Mr. Gonshak told her she could take her seat.

Later they were outside in the playground. Mr. Gonshak went to get the ball that looked like the

planet Earth. It was missing.

Mr. Gonshak was very upset. He asked everybody in the class if they had seen it.

"Maybe Chip took it with him to the Bermuda Triangle," said Keith. "Isn't that where everything disappears?"

"Why don't *you* disappear?" yelled Justin.

Mr. Gonshak went to talk to the principal and a group of teachers. "What's he saying?" asked Chip.

"I don't know," said Justin. "He's got the microphone off."

Chip slipped off his jeans and shirt and handed them to Justin. "Here. Hold these. I'll go invisible."

Justin stood there with Chip's clothes in his hands, feeling pretty stupid. He felt even stupider when Charlene came up to him and asked him what he was doing.

A few seconds later, the clothes jumped out of Justin's hands. "Turn around, Charlene! I'm naked," said Chip.

"You're invisible," said Charlene with her hands on her hips.

"Turn around!" hissed Chip. Charlene turned around. Chip quickly slipped his clothes back on.

"The teachers are really mad that the ball is gone. It cost a lot of money. And Ms. Gerber said yes to a date with Mr. Gonshak," said Chip. "Also, Mrs. Gumbel, our old first-grade teacher, is pregnant."

"Chip Stone, you've been eavesdropping!" exclaimed Charlene. "That's terrible. Did the teachers say anything about me?"

"Yeah, they said you're a P-E-T."

"The teacher's pet? Me?" Charlene preened.

"No, Pest Even to Teachers," said Chip.

Charlene pouted.

"He was just kidding," said
Justin. Then he explained how he
heard teachers' secrets with his transistor. "See. I can sometimes find
out things people don't want me to.
So can Chip. He just goes invisible
by taking his clothes off. It makes us
special."

"What's so special about eavesdropping and making up stupid jokes that make me feel bad?" said Charlene.

Chip scratched his shirt. "I didn't mean to make you feel bad."

"You guys should be using your powers for good, not evil."

"Charlene, we're not superheroes," said Chip. Justin nodded his head.

"I know," said Charlene. "But Justin can read lips and not everybody can do that. And Chip, well, *you're* certainly different."

"Right. We could call ourselves Two Weirdos for Peace and Justice," said Chip.

Justin laughed.

Charlene didn't.

"We could help kids who are in trouble," she said. "I got it! We could call ourselves Invisible Inc. The company that rights wrongs."

"What's this 'we'? What can *you* do?"

"I'm the one who thought of it," said Charlene. "Besides, you need a girl in your club. It's the law."

"She may be right," said Justin.

That afternoon, they went to Chip's house to get organized. "We need business cards," said Charlene, "to let people know that we're ready to help them."

Justin sat down at Chip's computer. Charlene dictated.

Justin tapped in her words. He printed them out on a business card.

```
INVISIBLE INC.
WE RIGHT WRONGS.
COME TO US WITH YOUR PROBLEMS.
WE CAN HELP.
```

It floated in the air. Chip was holding it without gloves on.

"I think we should write it in real invisible ink," said Charlene, peering at it over Chip's shoulder.

"Yeah? And where do we find invisible ink?" asked Justin.

"In the refrigerator," said Charlene. "Lemon juice looks invisible when you write with it. But if you hold it next to something warm, it shows up."

"Neat!" said Chip and Justin together.

Chip went to the refrigerator. He moved some hot dogs out of the way to get to the lemons. "You know, guys, this is the first time since the accident that I haven't felt like a weirdo."

Suddenly, Charlene screamed. "One of your hot dogs is running away."

A raw hot dog floated inches above the floor.

"That's just Max," said Chip. Max was Chip's dog. "He fell into the pool with me," said Chip. "But see? Part of his tail didn't get dipped."

Justin could see a little brown spot of a tail.

Chunks of hot dog mixed with dog saliva in midair. "Hey, this is neat," said Charlene. "It's kind of like a science experiment."

"It's kind of disgusting," said Justin. He took the lemons from Chip and started to squeeze out invisible ink. It took a lot of lemons, but Invisible Inc. was now official.

CHAPTER THREE
A Salamander Hostage

Chip, Justin, and Charlene handed out their business cards before school the next day.

Keith Broder took one. He laughed at it. "It's a blank card."

"Hold it up to something warm," said Chip.

Keith held it close to a light bulb. "What's this Invisible Inc.? Kids can't be incorporated."

"Yes, they can. Can't they Mr. Gonshak?" said Charlene.

"I think it's very nice that you children are helping Chip," said Mr. Gonshak.

"We're not doing it to help Chip," said Justin impatiently. "Chip and me and Charlene. *We* help people in trouble."

"Chip, Charlene, and *I*," corrected Mr. Gonshak. "Class, I am still very upset that the ball is missing from the playground. If anybody knows anything about this, please tell me. The principal, Ms. Maccarone, and I will not rest until we find out who took that ball. That ball is school property."

Chip passed a note to Charlene and Justin.

Maybe that's our first case. Invisible Inc. will find the ball and SAVE THE DAY!

Charlene and Justin nodded.

Mary raised her hand. Mary almost never raised her hand.

Mr. Gonshak called on her.

"I have a confession to make," whispered Mary. "I did it."

"Did what?" asked Mr. Gonshak.

Mary looked at the floor. "I took the ball," Mary stammered.

Mr. Gonshak stared at her. "Mary, *you*? Where is it?"

Mary's eyes were wide. "I . . . uh . . . I stuck it with my pen and made a hole in it, and then I buried it. I don't remember where."

"Mary!" Mr. Gonshak exclaimed. "That was a terrible thing to do. And so unlike you. Why did you do it?"

Mary wouldn't answer.

"I want to see you after school," said Mr. Gonshak.

Chip wrote a note and passed it to Charlene and Justin. *There goes our case.*

Charlene wrote back. *No! I'm sure Mary didn't do it. She needs our help.*

Justin nodded.

So did Chip. But nobody could see.

At lunchtime, Invisible Inc. asked
Mary if they could talk to her.

"I don't think so," said Mary.
Charlene held one of their cards up
to a warm dish of macaroni. Slowly,
INVISIBLE INC. WE RIGHT WRONGS.
became clear.

"You need us," said Charlene.

"No! Leave me alone," said Mary.
She ran away.

"That's great," said Justin. "Our first customer runs away. Invisible Inc. scores a big fat zero."

"Follow her, Chip," said Charlene. "Something is wrong."

Chip slipped off his clothes and went invisible. He followed Mary.

He was gone quite a while. When he came back, he put his clothes back on. "You won't believe what that stinker Keith Broder is doing to Mary."

"What?" Justin and Charlene asked.

"Remember that salamander that Mary brought for show-and-tell?"

"Dingbat," said Justin.

"Doormat," said Chip. "Well, Keith stuck the ball with his pen, and Mary saw him. But he's holding Doormat hostage and making Mary take the blame."

"Oh, poor Dingbat," said Justin.

"It's not Dingbat. It's Doormat," said Charlene and Chip together.

"We can't let him get away with this," said Charlene. She started to march across the lunchroom to make Keith confess.

Justin grabbed her. "Wait," he said. "He'll just deny it. We've got to trap him."

"How?" asked Chip.

Justin tapped his transistor. "I've got a plan," he whispered.

CHAPTER FOUR
High Fives

"I want to talk to you," Justin said to Keith during recess.

"Yeah, you and who else? Is that invisible kid with you?" Keith asked.

"No, I'm alone," said Justin. Justin backed against the wall.

"How do I know Chip's not invisible right behind you?" said Keith.

"You've got me backed in a corner," said Justin. "If Chip were behind me, I'd be squashing him."

"I like squished chips," said Keith. "What do you want? Or can't you hear me. Do you want me to talk louder?"

"No," said Justin, tapping the transistor around his neck. "I can

hear you. I know the wrong person is getting the blame for ruining our ball. You did it."

"Did Mary tell you?" asked Keith.

Justin nodded, but didn't say anything.

"There's nothing you can do about it," said Keith. "Mary is never in trouble. Mr. Gonshak won't do anything to her. That's why I picked on her. But she's in big trouble now for telling you. She'll never get her salamander back."

Keith shoved Justin. He glared back at him. "Don't try to follow me," he warned.

Justin stayed where he was.

Last year the PTO had paid to have a giant sandbox built for the kindergartners. Keith went to the sandbox. He shoved a little of the top of the sand to the side. There was Mary's pet salamander in its cage. A ripped giant ball was underneath the cage.

Chip grabbed the salamander and ran.

"Hey!" shouted Keith. All he could see was a cage floating across the playground. Chip handed the cage to Mary. Mary's mouth opened into a big O. Doormat had just flown across the playground into her hands.

Justin ran up to Keith. "You picked on the wrong person, dodo. Everything you said to me is on tape. This isn't my transistor. It's a tape recorder."

"Why, you little twerp!" said Keith. He tried to grab the transistor from around Justin's neck.

Suddenly, invisible hands
grabbed Keith.

Keith tried to punch Chip, but
only got air.

"What's going on?" demanded Mr.
Gonshak.

"Keith has something to say to
you," said Charlene.

Keith crossed his arms over his
chest. He shook his head.

Justin tapped the tape recorder
around his neck. "Would you like me
to play my tape for Mr. Gonshak?"
he asked.

Mr. Gonshak looked down and
saw the deflated ball. "What's *this*
doing here?" he asked.

Keith sighed. He knew he was
caught. "I did it," he said. "I was just
playing with my pen, and it slipped.
Mary didn't do it. She just said that
to be nice." Mary stroked her
salamander's cage.

"You're going straight to the principal's office," said Mr. Gonshak. He looked at Justin and Charlene. "I'm glad to finally know the truth. Maybe the ball can be fixed. Did you kids have anything to do with finding it?"

"Invisible Inc. saved the day," said Charlene.

Mr. Gonshak smiled. He took Keith to the principal's office.

Chip came back with his baseball cap and his clothes on. He was breathing hard. His shirt went in and out.

"I don't know how to thank you," said Mary in a shy voice.

Justin grinned. "Just speak up," he said. "It's hard for me to hear you when you mumble."

"And always remember to call on Invisible Inc. when help is nowhere to be seen," said Charlene.

Justin and Chip tried to give each other a high five, but they missed each other's hands.

Finally their hands touched, and they gave each other a big handshake. "There's still work to be done," said Charlene, putting her hand on top of Justin's.

"Yeah," said Justin. "We've got to work on our high fives. It's hard to give a high five to an invisible hand."

"Nothing's too hard for Invisible Inc.," said Charlene.

Justin grinned. He couldn't see it, but he was sure that Chip was grinning, too.

INVISIBLE INC.

The
Mystery of the
Missing Dog

To Ginger — The original Invisible–Visible Dog
— E.L.

In Memory of the Amazing June Grammer
— D.B.

The
Mystery of the
Missing Dog

by **Elizabeth Levy**

Illustrated by **Denise Brunkus**

Meet Invisible Inc.

Except for his tail, Chip's dog, Max, was invisible! So was Chip. But at least Chip wore clothes.

Last summer, Chip and Max were in a cave. They fell into a pool of water. When they came out, they were both invisible. Chip's clothes were invisible, too.

Soon Chip's family, his friends, and almost everyone in Chip's town got used to Chip. But no one except his good friends, Charlene and Justin, knew about his invisible clothes. With them, Chip could go totally invisible. Chip kept them in his backpack.

Justin had a hearing loss, and he could read lips. He looked at things very carefully. He often noticed things that others didn't. Charlene was very good at figuring things out. Together, the three of them started Invisible Inc. to solve mysteries. They right wrongs others don't see.

And just for fun, the kids write their notes with invisible ink!

CHAPTER 1
Where's That Max?

"Here, Max!" shouted Chip. Chip and his friends were going to take Chip's dog to the dog show. But where was he?

Suddenly, the TV went on by itself. And it was LOUD! Programs flashed across the screen.

"Max has the remote again!" said Chip.

"There it is!" shouted Justin.

The remote was floating in the air.

Justin jumped at the remote, but he could not get it. The remote flew across the room — followed by a little brown dot.

Charlene held out her hands.

"I've got him!" she shouted.

She handed the remote to Chip.

"Bad dog," she said to Max.

"He may not know how to use the remote control, but he does have a new trick for the dog show," said Chip.

Chip put a mitten in a hat, then clapped his hands. The mitten flew out of the hat and across the room. It was followed by the brown wagging dot.

"That's neat!" said Charlene. "The judges will love it."

"But the judges won't be able to see him," said Justin.

Chip was sad. "You're right. The judges won't give a prize to a dog they can't see."

"We can dye Max," said Charlene. "We can use food coloring."

Charlene mixed the food coloring, and Chip put Max in the tub. Brown water flew everywhere.

Now Max was visible. He was a deep chocolate brown.

"I hope he doesn't lick this stuff off," said Justin.

At the park was a huge sign: K-9 FUN FEST.

Max wagged his tail. He loved to be with other dogs.

Chip, Charlene, and Justin met Mary and Sandy, two girls from their class.

"Do you have a dog?" Justin asked.

Mary shook her head. "We just came to watch."

"My father is allergic to dogs," said Sandy.

Max's tail wagged. Chip held his leash tighter. A huge Doberman pinscher barked.

"Watch it!" said the boy who was holding the big dog's leash.

Chip pulled Max's leash. It wrapped around Mary's legs and she fell on the big dog.

"Be careful," said the boy. "You'll
hurt my champion!"

Mary looked scared.

"Your dog could have hurt Mary,"
said Chip.

"My dog is a purebred," said
the boy. "And I can see that yours
is not."

"Chip's dog may not be a pure-bred, but he has a pure heart," said Charlene.

"My dog is a champion. She always wins," said the boy. "She can do anything that your dog can do — but better."

"Well, *this* dog can disappear," said Charlene. "Can your dog do that?"

While the children talked, the two dogs licked each other. And Max started to disappear!

The boy was very surprised. He walked away, dragging his dog behind him.

"What happened to that dog?" a woman shouted. She had bright-red hair and wore purple clothes.

"He's invisible," said Charlene.

"Amazing!" said the woman. A low
growl came from under her cape. A
tiny dog with big ears peeked out.

"Amazing!" the woman said again. Then she walked away.

"She's strange," said Justin.

"We'll have to dye Max again," said Chip.

"I'm hungry," Charlene said. "Let's have lunch first."

Charlene, Justin, and Chip walked to the food stand. On the way, they passed the snobby boy with his big dog, the strange woman with her little dog, and Sandy and Mary with no dog at all.

The children ordered nachos. A tortilla chip with gooey cheese on it dropped to the ground.

"It's okay, Max. You can eat it," said Chip.

But the nacho just lay on the ground.

"Why isn't Max eating the nacho?" Justin asked.

Chip tugged on Max's leash. It was slack.

"He's not here!" Chip shouted. "Someone took Max!"

CHAPTER 2
Lost — One Dog
You Can't See

Chip, Justin, and Charlene searched the park for Max. They called his name again and again. But no little brown tail came wagging.

They asked the snobby boy, the strange woman, Sandy, and Mary if they knew where Max could be. They all said no.

"This is a case for Invisible Inc.!" said Charlene.

"Right," groaned Chip. "We can put up posters: 'Lost — One Dog You Can't See!' I suppose you'll want to write the posters in invisible ink, too."

"Don't be silly," said Charlene.
"Justin can make great posters."

Justin was a very good artist. He
made posters that showed Max's
brown tail. The large, red letters
announced:

Chip, Charlene, and Justin put
the signs up all over the park.
Justin put one on a tree and noticed
another poster nearby.

"Hey, look at this!" he said. "That lady was a magician." He pointed to a picture of the woman with the red hair. AMAZING GRACE read the poster. CALL TODAY! WE DO MAGIC SHOWS FOR BIRTHDAY PARTIES.

Charlene started to write something down on her pad.

"What are you doing?" Chip asked.

"Taking her address and phone number," said Charlene. "I might want a magician at my next birthday party."

By the end of the day, nobody had turned in an invisible dog with a dot of a tail.

On their way out of the park, Chip, Justin, and Charlene ran into the snobby boy from the dog show.

"Have you seen our dog, Max, anywhere?" asked Charlene. "He seemed to like your dog. Maybe he followed her."

"You keep your dog away from my Millie," warned the boy. "I don't like her licking all of that food coloring." He tugged on Millie's leash and left.

"I think he knows where Max is," said Chip. "I'm going to follow him."

Chip ran behind a tree. He put on his invisible clothes. Chip's invisibility could come in handy at times like this.

Fifteen minutes later, Chip returned, huffing.

"Well, I didn't find Max," said Chip. "But I did find out that boy's name. I heard his mother call for him from her car — William Watson the Third."

"But did you find any clues about Max?" asked Justin.

"Not exactly," said Chip. "But I don't trust that William Watson the Third. I know he has something to do with Max disappearing."

Charlene frowned. "A good detective doesn't jump to conclusions."

"She's right," said Justin. "Just because he wants his dog to win doesn't mean he did it."

"But if he didn't," asked Chip as he put his visible clothes back on, "who did?"

CHAPTER 3
Amazing Dog Tricks

On their way home, the members of Invisible Inc. saw Mary. She was carrying a shopping bag from the dog show.

"I saw your posters," said Mary. "Did you find Max yet?"

"No," said Charlene, looking sad. "We've looked everywhere for him."

"It would be amazing if you find him," said Mary. "There are so many dogs here, and you can't even see Max."

"What did you say?" Justin asked.

Mary turned to face him. She knew Justin could read her lips better if she looked straight at him.

"I said it would be amazing if you found him," repeated Mary.

"Amazing . . ." Justin said to himself.

Mary looked at him strangely. "I've got to go," she said, clutching her shopping bag. "I hope you find Max."

"I don't see what's so amazing," complained Charlene. "We haven't found Max, and we don't even have any clues."

"Who would want an invisible dog?" Justin asked slowly. "Use your head."

Chip scratched his head and thought.

Suddenly, Charlene's eyes lit up. "Amazing Grace!" she shouted.

"Right!" said Justin. "A magician would have a million uses for an invisible dog. I'll bet she has Max."

"But how can we find out for sure?" asked Charlene.

"Let's go to her house and pretend that we want to hire her for a birthday party," said Chip. He turned to Charlene. "You have her address, right?"

Charlene took out her pad. She had used her special Invisible Inc. pen, filled with lemon juice, to write the address.

"We need something warm so we can read it," said Justin. He ran back to the park and bought a hot chocolate at the refreshment stand.

Charlene held the paper over the steam from the cup. As soon as the address appeared, they were off.

Amazing Grace lived in a very strange house. It was painted pink and had shutters with blue stars.

Charlene rang the doorbell. Amazing Grace answered the door, carrying her Chihuahua and a shopping bag of dog food from the show.

"Yes?" said the woman.

"We're having a birthday party," said Chip, "and we saw your poster in the park. Can you do tricks with dogs in your magic show?"

Amazing Grace laughed as she invited them in.

"Can I do tricks with dogs? Watch this!" she said. "Merlin — fetch!"

The little dog jumped on Charlene's shoulder and pulled a quarter out from behind her ear.

"Wow!" said Charlene. "How did you teach him to do that?"

"A good magician never reveals her secrets," said Grace, smiling. "Now, when are you planning to have this party?"

Before Charlene could answer, Justin interrupted.

"May I have that?" he asked, pointing to the shopping bag on the floor.

The magician smiled at him. She took out several cans of dog food from the bag and turned it inside out.

"Whoops! It's not empty," said Grace. She pulled out a bunch of

paper flowers and handed them to Justin.

"That was great!" said Chip.

"Thanks," said Justin, as he returned the flowers, "but I just want the bag. Thanks again!" he shouted as he ran out of the house. Chip and Charlene followed.

"What's gotten into you?" asked Charlene. "Why did you want that bag?"

"There's no time to explain," said Justin. "I think I know who took Max. We've been barking up the wrong tree!"

CHAPTER 4
Canine Clues

"At last. A real clue!" Justin said, pointing to the shopping bag. The words *Debbie's Delicious Dog Food* were printed on the side. "We've seen this shopping bag before."

"We have?" said Charlene and Chip together.

Justin nodded. "This is the same shopping bag that Mary had. Mary doesn't have a dog. She has a salamander. Why would she buy dog food for a salamander?"

"Because she has Max!" exclaimed Charlene.

"Exactly!" declared Justin.

Charlene started down the street. "Come on. Let's go to Mary's house."

"Wait," said Justin. "We have to have a plan."

"We don't have time for a plan," said Chip. "It's getting dark. I have to find Max."

They ran to Mary's house and rang the bell. Mary came to the door.

"Hi, guys," she said. "Any luck finding Max?"

"No," said Justin, spotting the shopping bag on the floor. He picked it up and lifted out a can of dog food.

"Why did you buy dog food?" asked Justin.

"Uh — I — I — a friend asked me to buy it for her new dog," Mary stammered, turning red.

"We think you bought it for an invisible dog," Charlene blurted out.

Justin rolled his eyes. He knew that a good detective doesn't accuse a suspect until all of the evidence is in.

"Max isn't here," said Mary. "You
can search the house if you want to."

Charlene and Justin headed for
the den, but Chip sank down on a
chair. He knew Max wasn't there. If
Max were there, he would have
come running.

"I may never see Max again," said
Chip.

"We're sorry, Mary," said Justin.
"We shouldn't have blamed you."

"I'm sure Max is all right," said Mary.

"I'm not," Chip said, standing up. "I guess I should go home." For a moment he looked hopeful. "Maybe Max is waiting there for me."

"Good idea," said Mary, trying to cheer him up.

Chip raced down the street, with Justin and Charlene following close behind. But when they got to Chip's house, there was no wagging tail. There was no Max at all.

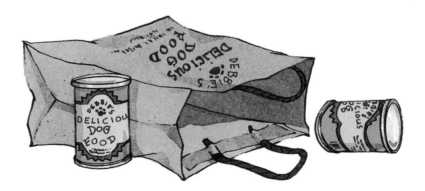

CHAPTER 5
Lost and Found

The next day, Chip was almost too unhappy to go to the dog show. "But you have to go," said Charlene. "Max just might show up there."

When they got there, as always, Charlene was hungry. "Come on," she said. "Let's go get a hot dog."

"Who could eat a hot dog at a time like this?" asked Chip.

Justin sighed. "You go, Charlene. I'll stay with Chip. Bring me back a hot dog, too."

Charlene bought the hot dogs and stopped at a souvenir stand on the way back. William Watson the Third strutted by with Millie at his side. "Did your friend ever find his dog?" he asked.

Charlene shook her head.

"Too bad," William said. "I guess he's a *no show*."

"That's mean," said Charlene. "You wouldn't like it if someone took Millie."

William Watson the Third looked a little embarrassed. He picked up a stuffed rabbit. When he squeezed it, it barked. "I bet Millie would love fetching this," said William.

"Hey, I'm buying that," said Mary's friend, Sandy. She grabbed the toy and paid for it.

"She sure is in a hurry," said William.

Charlene stared at Sandy's back. Taking out her fountain pen, she wrote on a napkin in invisible ink and gave it to William Watson the Third.

"Will you run and give this to
Chip and Justin?" she asked.

William looked at the napkin. "It's
blank."

"Please do it," Charlene begged.

"Why should I do you a favor?" William Watson the Third asked.

"Think how you would feel if someone took Millie," said Charlene.

"I'd hate it," said William Watson the Third. He took the paper.

"Take these to them, too," said Charlene as she gave him the hot dogs. "I've got to run. They'll know what to do." Charlene took off after Sandy.

William Watson the Third brought the napkin and hot dogs to Justin and Chip.

"What's this?" asked Justin, taking the napkin. "Another joke?"

"Your friend Charlene asked me to give it to you," said William. "She said you'd know what to do." He handed Chip the hot dogs. "I hope you find your dog."

"Thanks," said Chip. "Thanks a lot." William smiled a little and walked away, with Millie following close behind.

Justin held the napkin over the heat of the hot dog. The words

appeared.

"Let's go!" shouted Justin.

Chip was already ahead of him.

When they got to Sandy's house, Charlene was hiding behind a tree.

"Do you see Max?" Chip whispered urgently.

Charlene shook her head. "No. But listen."

"I don't hear anything," said Justin.

But Chip heard a bark. "It's Max!" he said excitedly. He ran to the front door before Justin could stop him.

Sandy's father answered the bell.

"Excuse me," said Chip, trying to be polite. "But I think you may have my dog."

"We don't allow dogs in our home," said Sandy's dad. He sneezed and rubbed at his red eyes. "I'm allergic to them."

Suddenly, a bark came from inside the house. Sandy came to the door carrying the stuffed rabbit she had bought at the show. "It's my new toy," she said. "It's a rabbit that barks."

Sandy's father sneezed again. "I seem to be allergic even to toy rabbits that bark like dogs."

Chip looked discouraged. "Another false alarm."

Just as the door was closing, Chip heard another bark.

Chip ran to Justin and Charlene. "I know Max's bark. That *is* him in there—somewhere. I've got to go invisible. You and Charlene ring the doorbell again."

"What am I going to say?" asked Justin.

"Say anything," said Chip, quickly changing into his invisible clothes. "Just give me a chance to get inside."

Charlene and Justin rang the
doorbell. "Hello. Can I help you with
something?" Sandy's mother asked
them.

"Uh . . . we're collecting money for
animal rescue," Charlene said
quickly. "We find lost animals."

Sandy's mother smiled. "How
nice. I'll get some change."

While they waited by the open door, Chip slipped inside. Moments later, a streak of a brown tail came flying out of the house.

"What was that?" asked Sandy's mother.

Sandy ran down the stairs and out of the house.

"Excuse us," said Charlene. She and Justin ran after Sandy.

Chip was waiting behind a tree. A little brown dot wagged back and forth in Chip's arms. "Good boy!" said Chip, hugging Max tightly. "Good dog!"

Sandy heard Max barking and saw the brown dot.

"I'm sorry," she said. "I just took him as an experiment. I thought maybe my dad wouldn't be allergic to an invisible dog.

"I asked Mary to buy some dog food for Max yesterday and then I was going to bring him back. But Mary told me how worried you all were. I was scared that you would be angry with me. But honestly, I would have brought him back to you tonight."

"By then he would have missed the whole dog show," said Charlene.

Chip looked down at the wagging brown dot. "He doesn't have a chance. The judges can't see him. And there's no time to use food coloring on him now."

"Wait a minute," said Charlene. "Max can pull a rabbit out of a hat."

"He can do what?" asked Chip.

Charlene explained her plan. Chip giggled and looked at Sandy.

"We'll have to borrow your stuffed rabbit," he said.

"Of course," said Sandy. "It's the least I can do."

They ran back to the dog show. Chip walked into the ring with Max. To everyone else, it looked as if Chip was walking a pretend dog on a trick leash.

"What's this?" asked a judge.

"This is my dog, Max," said Chip.

The judge knelt down. His hand became wet as Max slobbered kisses on his knuckles.

"It *is* a dog," said the judge.

"And he's officially entered," said another judge, looking at her list.

"It's highly unusual," said one judge to the other.

They read their rule book.

"There is no rule against invisible dogs," said the first judge.

Max trotted smartly by Chip's side, heeling perfectly when Chip stopped. Justin, Charlene, Sandy, and Mary all cheered loudly. William Watson the Third even gave Chip a thumbs-up sign.

Chip put his baseball cap down in the center of the ring.

"Presenting the Amazing Max!" he cried.

He clapped his hands. Quick as a blink, a brown dot shot across the ring and hovered over the hat.

"Abracadabra!" shouted Chip.

The rabbit jumped out of the hat
and floated through the air, landing
at the feet of the judges.

Max and Chip won first prize in
the Silly Dog Trick category. After
the show, Chip carried his blue
ribbon over to his friends.

"I guess you just can't keep an
invisible dog down," he said proudly.

"Your dog is amazing," said a
familiar voice.

Chip turned to see Amazing Grace and her Chihuahua. She handed Chip her business card.

"Perhaps we can do business together," she said.

Chip reached into his pocket and handed her an official Invisible Inc. card.

"It's blank," said Amazing Grace.

"It's not blank. It's invisible," said Charlene.

"Invisible Inc. at your service," added Justin.

Amazing Grace took the card and smiled. "Amazing," she whispered.

INVISIBLE INC.

The Snack Attack Mystery

To Nan, the master snacker
— E.L.

For Kate, Queen of Snacks
— D.B.

The
Snack Attack
Mystery

by **Elizabeth Levy**

Illustrated by **Denise Brunkus**

Chip fell into a strange pool of water. Now Chip is invisible! Justin knows how to read lips because of his hearing loss. Charlene is sometimes bossy, but always brave. Together they are Invisible Inc.— and they solve mysteries!

CHAPTER 1
A Very, Very Weird Class

Chip stood very still. He tried to be quiet. But his stomach growled. He hoped nobody could hear it. He didn't want anyone to find him.

Chip and his friends were playing hide-and-seek. They had to make new rules because he was invisible:
(1) Chip couldn't hide behind trees.
(2) Chip couldn't hold his breath.
(3) Chip couldn't leave the playground.

Chip's stomach growled again.

"I think I heard something," said Charlene. She waved her hands in the air. She hoped to find Chip first.

Chip tried to make his stomach quiet. But he was really hungry.

"I hear him!" Charlene shouted. Charlene lunged. She came up with nothing but air.

Her little brother, Stanley, laughed. "You couldn't even catch *me*. And *I'm* not even invisible."

Stanley twirled by. He almost twirled right into Chip.

"This isn't a game for kindergartners," Charlene said to her brother.

"You don't have to be mean to him," said Justin.

Charlene rolled her eyes. "You don't know him. Now, I've forgotten where I heard Chip's stomach."

Just then, their teacher, Mr. Gonshak, came outside with a new girl.

"Boys and girls, gather around,"
said Mr. Gonshak. "This is Dawn
Park. She is new to our class.
Charlene, why don't you let Dawn
play in your game?"

Mr. Gonshak went to talk to the
other teachers.

"Hi, Dawn," said Charlene. "We're playing hide-and-seek. You can help Sandy and Justin and me catch Chip. I know he's close. His noisy stomach is going to give him away."

Charlene waved her arms in the air. Justin and Sandy waved, too.

"What are you doing?" Dawn asked.

"We're looking for Chip," said Sandy. "He's around here some-where."

Dawn turned around. "I don't see any hiding places," she said.

"Chip doesn't need a hiding place. He's invisible," explained Justin.

Dawn thought that the children were making fun of her. She hated going to a new school. She hated not having friends.

Just then Chip's stomach growled again. Charlene heard it. She grabbed the air and got Chip's arm.

"I got him!" she shouted.

"This is so embarrassing!" said Chip.

The air around his face got red.

"Over here, Dawn!" shouted Charlene. "We got him."

Dawn looked at Charlene. Charlene was talking to somebody who wasn't there.

"Isn't she a little old to have an imaginary friend?" Dawn asked Justin.

"What?" said Justin.

"Isn't she a little old to have an imaginary friend?" Dawn shouted.

"You have to face me. I can read lips," said Justin.

"Dawn, meet Chip," Charlene said.

She pointed to the air beside her.

Dawn started to cry. She thought that everyone was teasing her.

Just then Mr. Gonshak blew his whistle.

"It's time to come in," he said.
"Chip, go change into your regular
clothes."

"Good," said a voice next to
Dawn. "It's snack time. I'm starv-
ing."

Dawn jumped. "Who said that?"

"Me! I'm Chip!" said Chip.

He reached out and shook Dawn's
hand. She felt something — but she
saw nothing. Dawn screamed.

"What's wrong?" shouted Mr.
Gonshak.

"The new girl is afraid of Chip!"
said Keith. He laughed.

"Dawn, we'll tell you about Chip during snack time," said Mr. Gonshak.

"Mr. Gonshak's hungry," said Justin. "He was just talking to the teachers about being on a diet."

"How do you know what he said all the way over there?" asked Dawn.

"I've got ways," said Justin proudly.

Justin's teacher spoke into a microphone. It made his teacher's voice sound louder just to Justin. Mr. Gonshak was always forgetting to turn it off.

Dawn blinked. Everyone was trying to confuse her.

The boys and girls walked into the classroom. They went to their cubbies to get their snacks. Except for Dawn.

"I didn't bring a snack," said Dawn. "No one told me to."

"You can have some of mine," said Sandy.

But Sandy couldn't find her snack. "Hey!" she shouted. "My snack is gone! I had a bag of nuts and raisins."

"Mine is gone, too!" said Charlene.

"So is mine!" said Justin.

His mom had packed his favorite — chocolate-covered nuts.

Just then Dawn screamed. She
saw a shirt, pants, and shoes — but
no head or hands. Chip had walked
in the door.

Chip went to his cubby.

"My snack! Somebody took my
snack!" he said.

"This is a case for Invisible Inc.,"
said Justin loudly.

"What's Invisible Inc.?" asked
Dawn. She was almost crying. It was
her first day in a brand-new school,
and nothing made sense at all.

Mr. Gonshak tried to explain. "One of the boys in this class is a little different. We have gotten used to Chip. But it can be a shock when you first meet him. Chip, please tell Dawn what happened to you."

Chip walked to the front of the class, brushing against Dawn. Dawn shivered as if he were a ghost. Chip told her what had happened to him.

Charlene waved her arm in the air. "Mr. Gonshak! Mr. Gonshak! Let me tell Dawn about Invisible Inc."

"It's a club with a boy you can't see, a boy who can't hear, and a girl who bosses everybody around!" Keith shouted out.

The class laughed.

Mr. Gonshak frowned at Keith. He pointed to the bulletin board.

"Keith, remember our class rules. No shouting out in class. No calling each other names." Mr. Gonshak turned to the class. "What is our motto?"

"Respect for ourselves and each other!" said the class.

Dawn felt more confused than ever. And she didn't even know the class rules.

"We have to find out how many snacks were stolen," said Charlene. She walked to the front of the class. "I'll pass out our cards. Write down if your snack was stolen. I'll make a chart."

Charlene always had a stack of Invisible Inc. business cards with her.

"I'll help," said Sandy. She gave a card to Dawn. Dawn turned it over.

"It's blank," she said.

"Hold it up to the lightbulb by the gerbil's cage," explained Chip. "It's written in lemon juice."

Chip reached out to take the card from Dawn. Dawn drew back. She was afraid to touch Chip's invisible hands.

The gerbils were in a cage at the side of the room, and there was a light above the cage.

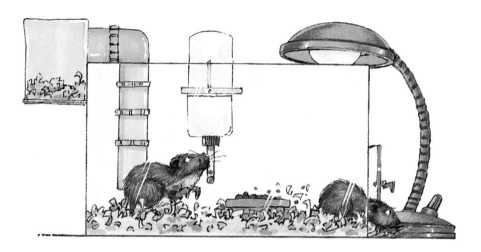

"Have you met Hola and Jambo yet?" asked Chip. "*Hola* and *Jambo* mean hello in Spanish and Swahili."

Dawn looked at the gerbils.

"Hey!" said Dawn. "One of them is getting out!"

Chip laughed and pushed Hola back into the cage.

"They're always doing that," he said.

Dawn held the card over the light. Slowly words began to appear:

INVISIBLE INC.

WE RIGHT WRONGS

COME TO US WITH YOUR PROBLEMS.

WE CAN HELP.

CHAPTER 2
Nuts

In the cafeteria, Justin made a chart of all the snacks that had been stolen, including: Mary's nuts; Sandy's bag of raisins and nuts; Chip's peanut-butter cookies.

Justin looked up from his chart. Dawn was on the lunch line. Spaghetti was the main dish. For dessert, there was a chocolate sundae with nuts, and pudding. Dawn took pudding.

Dawn sat by herself. She looked over at the kids from Invisible Inc. Chip swallowed a strand of spaghetti. It looked like a worm flying through the air. Everybody could see the food in Chip's mouth. Chip's friends were used to it. But Dawn was not. She pushed her spaghetti

away. She wasn't hungry anymore.

Justin watched Dawn.

"Remember how Dawn was late for recess?" he said to Charlene and Chip. "Maybe she was sneaking around our classroom—"

"And taking our snacks!" said Charlene.

"She isn't eating much of her lunch," said Justin.

"Wait a minute," said Chip. "Just because she's new doesn't mean she's the thief. I think we should give her a chance."

Dawn carried her tray to cleanup. She passed Chip just as he was taking a big bite of chocolate sundae with nuts on top. A nut in a gooey puddle disappeared into his shirt. Dawn almost dropped her tray. Her pudding plopped right on Justin's head.

"Sorry," said Dawn.

"You weren't very hungry," said Justin, picking the pudding out of his hair.

"You should have had the chocolate sundae. It's much better than the pudding," said Chip.

Dawn couldn't look at Chip. He was too scary.

"I'm allergic to chocolate and nuts," said Dawn.

She hurried away.

"Ah-ha!" said Charlene. "Did you see her tray? She hardly ate a bite. She stole our snacks. That's why she wasn't hungry."

Justin shook his head sadly.

"No, Charlene. It couldn't have been Dawn," he said. He pointed to his chart. "Almost two-thirds of the snacks stolen were nuts. And Dawn is allergic to nuts."

"Nuts!" said Charlene. "I thought we had our thief. Now we have to start all over."

CHAPTER 3
A Gross Job

All week, snacks disappeared from the classroom. Invisible Inc. was busy making up its chart. Justin pointed out that snacks were stolen during both morning *and* afternoon recess.

"At least it's an equal opportunity thief," said Mr. Gonshak when Invisible Inc. showed him the chart. He taped the chart up above the gerbils' cage.

DAY	TIME	STUDENTS WITH STOLEN SNACKS
MON.	A.M.	SANDY (NUTS & RAISINS), CHARLENE (CASHEWS), MARY (NUTS), CHIP (PEANUT BUTTER COOKIES), JUSTIN (CHOCOLATE-COVERED NUTS)
	P.M.	
TUES.	A.M.	
	P.M.	KEITH (ALMONDS), MARY (OATMEAL COOKIES)
WED.	A.M.	CHARLENE (YOGURT-COVERED RAISINS)
	P.M.	SANDY (BROWNIE W/NUTS)
THUR.	A.M.	
	P.M.	

During morning recess, the teachers gathered near the play fort. Mr. Gonshak left his microphone on by mistake again.

"Teacher Lite?" said Justin.

"What are you talking about?" asked Dawn.

"Shh," said Justin. "I think I'm on to something. It might be a clue. Go get Charlene and Chip."

Dawn ran to get Charlene and Chip. Charlene and Chip knew Justin was listening to something.

"What can you hear?" asked Chip.

"The teachers are dieting together," said Justin. "They will weigh themselves today. They are going to pick the Teacher Lite of the Month."

"What does that have to do with the stolen snacks?" asked Dawn.

Justin scratched his head. He didn't have an answer.

Back inside, Mary shouted, "Somebody's been in my desk!"

The floor around her desk was a mess. Papers had fallen everywhere.

"I'll bet your snack is missing,"
said Charlene.

"You're right," said Mary. "I had
saved my cookies from yesterday.
My favorites! Ginger snaps."

Justin saw something on the floor
next to Mary's desk. He got an
envelope and filled it with what he
found on the floor. He marked the
envelope EXHIBIT A.

Just then, Mr. Gonshak came
into the room.

"We had another snack attack!" said Sandy.

"Yeah, and the mighty detectives strike out again," said Keith.

"That's enough, Keith," said Mr. Gonshak, pointing again to the respect rules.

This time, when Mr. Gonshak asked for the class motto, Dawn could shout out with the others, "Respect for ourselves and each other."

Mr. Gonshak told the boys and girls to take out their reading books. Justin pretended to read, but he was really studying Mr. Gonshak. Mr. Gonshak seemed nervous lately. He couldn't sit still. He sharpened pencils. He walked up and down the classroom.

It must be the diet, Justin thought.

Mr. Gonshak tapped on the gerbils' cage. The gerbils squeaked. A teacher on a diet wasn't easy on anybody — even the gerbils.

It was time for library. The class was working on a project about weather.

Justin slipped a note to Charlene.

I found a clue!

Justin held up the envelope.

"Do you have a signed confession?" asked Charlene.

"No, but it's a real clue." Justin emptied the envelope on the table. "I found these all around Mary's desk," he said.

"Pencil shavings!" said Charlene. "Mr. Gonshak is always sharpening pencils."

"Yes," said Justin. "And I see another clue. Look at his beard."

Mr. Gonshak was talking to the librarian, Ms. Grace. His beard was going up and down. There were crumbs stuck in it.

"Oh, gross," said Charlene.

"I bet those are ginger snap crumbs in his beard. We need to get those crumbs," said Justin. He looked at Chip. "Put them in this envelope." The envelope was marked EXHIBIT B.

"I'm supposed to pick the crumbs out of Mr. Gonshak's beard?" asked Chip. He couldn't believe it.

"It's a tough job, but somebody has got to do it," said Charlene.

Chip sighed. He raised his hand and told the librarian that he had to go to the bathroom. Then he put on his invisible clothes and snuck back into the library.

Mr. Gonshak jumped.

"Ouch!" he said.

"What's wrong?" asked Ms. Grace.

"Are there mosquitoes around here?" asked Mr. Gonshak.

Mr. Gonshak waved his hand in front of his face. He accidentally hit Chip on the nose.

"Ouch!" said Chip.

"Ah-choo!" said Charlene loudly to cover up for Chip.

One by one the crumbs disappeared from Mr. Gonshak's beard.

Then Chip changed back into his regular clothes. He held out the envelope.

"I got them!" he said excitedly.

"Good," said Justin.

Later in the day, during science time, Justin asked the aide, Ms. Canning, if he could use the microscope.

"Sure," said Ms. Canning. "I'll be glad to help you."

She helped Justin put the crumbs under the microscope.

"Rice," said Ms. Canning.

Justin looked into the microscope. Charlene and Chip gathered around.

"Rice! Are you sure they're not cookie crumbs?" asked Justin.

"Oh, no," said Ms. Canning. "You can see the little husks from the rice kernel. This is rice. Like from those rice cakes Mr. Gonshak eats for lunch."

That afternoon, Mr. Gonshak proudly announced to the class that he had lost six pounds. He was named Teacher Lite of the Week. Invisible Inc. was wrong again.

CHAPTER 4
The Master Snacker

The next morning, the whole school went to the assembly room for the kindergarten show. It was a play about foods. Charlene's little brother, Stanley, was a turkey.

"The turkey plays a turkey," Charlene said to Chip.

During recess, Charlene looked for Stanley.

"You were a great turkey," Charlene said.

"Thanks," said Stanley. "Did you lose your snack today? You can share mine."

Stanley passed a can of nuts to Charlene. The can was labeled FANCY SALTED MIXED NUTS and it showed lots of cashews — her very favorites.

"Did Mom give you these?" she asked. "How come she didn't give these to me?"

Stanley shrugged.

"Maybe she knew somebody would steal yours," he said.

"Come on," said Chip. "Open the can. I want some, too."

Charlene twisted the lid. Suddenly, two yellow plastic snakes jumped out of the can and bopped her on the nose.

"I should have known!" Charlene shouted.

"Fooled you! Fooled you!" said Stanley. He skipped away with his friends.

"I can't believe I fell for that!"
Charlene said.

"My aunt once played that trick
on me," said Chip.

"Well, some detective you are,"
said Charlene. "Why didn't you warn
me?"

"I forgot about it," said Chip.

Charlene looked thoughtful. "That
brother of mine is such a sneak. I'll
bet that he's our snack thief."

"Who?" asked Justin and Chip.

"Stanley!" said Charlene. "He's
always having snack attacks at

home. Mom calls him the Master Snacker."

"Stanley?" said Justin. "Your little brother? You think he's been stealing the snacks in our classroom?"

"Kindergartners are so cute and little. A kindergartner could sneak into our room and nobody would notice," said Charlene.

Justin looked at Chip.

"How much skill does it take to sneak a snack?" asked Chip. "We have book buddies with the kindergarten this morning. We can check things out then."

Late in the morning, Mr. Gonshak's class went to the kindergarten class to read with their book buddies. Justin sat with Andrea, his book buddy. Andrea also had trouble hearing, and Justin was teaching her sign language. They were reading a book about caterpillars.

Andrea got up and went to her cubby hole.

"Where are you going?" Justin signed.

"Home," signed Andrea.

She pointed to the clock. Justin looked around. All the kindergartners were packing up to go home. Justin smacked his forehead with his palm.

"Morning kindergartners," he said.

Stanley put on his jacket.

"Bye-bye, Charlie-pie!" he said to his sister.

Charlene hated to be called Charlie-pie.

"You'll be a mud pie, Stanley," warned Charlene. "Just as soon as I come up with the proof that you're the one who's been taking our snacks!"

"Charlene," said Justin, "it wasn't Stanley. He's only here in the mornings. My chart shows that some of the snacks were taken in the afternoon."

"Are you sure?" Charlene asked.

"I'm sure," said Justin.

Charlene sighed. "I can't believe it. Invisible Inc. is wrong again. Where is Chip? Maybe we should just have a going-out-of-business sale."

Justin looked around. Chip was nowhere to be seen.

CHAPTER 5
An Inside Job

Back in the classroom, Dawn was staring at the top of her desk. She was holding something small, white, and round in her hand. The gerbils in the cage behind her were trying to escape again.

"Hey!" said Charlene. "That's a yogurt-covered raisin. That's my snack! What is it doing in your desk?"

"I don't know," said Dawn. "I just found it."

"Found it or took it!" said Charlene. She put her hands on her hips. "You're not allergic to raisins or yogurt. Maybe Invisible Inc. doesn't have to go out of business after all."

Dawn looked as if she wanted to crawl under her desk.

Charlene shouted. "Mr. Gonshak! Justin! Sandy! Mary! Everybody! I caught the thief. Invisible Inc. saves the day. It was Dawn, after all. I caught her with my snack in her hand."

Dawn's eyes started to fill with tears. "I didn't take it! Somebody put it in my desk. Nobody likes me. I wish I weren't me. I wish I were a big fat gerbil, like Hola and Jambo."

"The gerbils are fat because they've been eating our snacks," said a voice next to Dawn.

Dawn jumped.

"It's okay!" said the voice. "It's me — Chip. And Dawn's right. She didn't take the snacks. I came back here to hide while the classroom was empty. Hola and Jambo are to blame."

Justin ran to his desk and got the envelope marked EXHIBIT A.

"It's sawdust," he said. "Not

pencil shavings. Sawdust from the gerbil cage."

"Right!" said Chip. "It was the gerbils the whole time. They sneak out and look for food. Then they take it back to their nest to hide it under the sawdust. They dropped the yogurt raisin in Dawn's desk."

"So," said Charlene. "The snack attacks have been inside jobs. Very inside. Dawn, I'm sorry I accused you and made you cry. The next time we've got a case to solve, you can help us."

"Yeah, you're an honorary member of Invisible Inc.," said Chip.

Chip shook her hand. This time, Dawn wasn't afraid.

"Thanks!" said Dawn. "I can see that having an invisible friend can be good."

Dawn grinned. Now she had friends at her new school—and one of them was invisible.

INVISIBLE INC.

The
Creepy Computer
Mystery

*To the voices on the other end of
computer help lines everywhere*
—E.L.

For my sister, Karen
—D.B.

INVISIBLE INC.

The
Creepy Computer
Mystery

by **Elizabeth Levy**

Illustrated by **Denise Brunkus**

Chip fell into a strange pool of water. Now Chip is invisible. Justin knows how to read lips because of his hearing loss. Charlene is sometimes bossy, but always brave. Together they are Invisible Inc.—and they solve mysteries!

CHAPTER 1
Invitation to Doom

Justin sat at the computer. He tapped in his screen name, GonzoJust. The librarian, Ms. Grace, let him log in for the whole class. Today the class was going to go on-line with its favorite author, U.B. Spooks.

Justin loved to use the computer. Talking on the phone was hard for him because he couldn't hear well and he couldn't read lips over the phone. But on the computer, Justin didn't have to hear. He could read instead.

"Get your questions ready!" said Charlene.

"I want to ask about *Slime on the Playground*," said Chip. "That was awesome."

"You're invisible slime," Keith said to Chip. "I bet U.B. Spooks could write a book about you."

Chip gave Keith an angry look, but Keith didn't know. That was one of the problems with being invisible. Nobody could see your face when you were mad or sad.

"It's time. It's time!" shouted Justin.

The screen showed the cover of U.B. Spooks' newest book, *Poison in the Lunch Room.*

On-line Host: Good afternoon. We know you are eager to meet U.B. Spooks. But, please remember, U.B. Spooks might not be able to answer all questions.

U.B. Spooks: Hi, everybody out there!

Justin quickly typed in the first question. *Will you come to our school? We have an invisible boy here.*

But the words didn't appear on the monitor.

Justin frowned. Questions were getting through from other classes around the country. But not from theirs.

Question: If you weren't an author what would you be?

U.B. Spooks: That's a funny question. Because I'm not only an author. I have another job, but I like to keep it private.

Question: Where do you get your ideas?

U.B. Spooks: From everywhere. From everything I see and hear and from people all around me. I'm always looking for new ideas.

Question: What do the initials U.B. stand for?

U.B. Spooks: U.B. Spooks is my pen name. I guess I just like the sound of "ooo."

Question: Why do you use a pen name?

U.B. Spooks: I like to keep the two sides of my life separate. Nobody I

work with knows that I am an
author.

"What do you think the other job is?" asked Keith.

"Why aren't our questions getting in there?" asked Charlene.

"Give me time," said Justin. He banged on the keys. They were frozen.

"Whoops," said Justin. "Whoops" is not a word that anybody likes to hear around a computer.

"What's wrong?" asked Ms. Grace. Ms. Grace hated when anything went wrong with the library's computer.

"The keys are frozen," said Justin.

"But it's warm in here," said Charlene.

"Not really frozen. It just means that I can't type anything," said Justin.

"Maybe too many people are trying to get through," said Sandy.

"Won't we get to ask our questions?" asked Mary. "Maybe we should raise our hands."

Charlene put her hands on her hips. "Don't be silly, Mary. The author is on a computer somewhere. U.B. Spooks can't see us raise our hands!"

"I was making a joke," said Mary.

"The keys are okay now!" said Justin. He repeated his question.

Question: Would you like to come to a school where you'd meet an invisible boy?

Suddenly the screen went blank!

"Whoops!" Justin said again.

"I wish you would stop saying that!" said Charlene.

"What's wrong?" asked Ms. Grace.

"I don't know," said Justin. He

tapped the escape button, but nothing worked. Meanwhile, Chip was sulking in the corner. That was another problem with being invisible. Nobody noticed when you were sulking.

"You've got to get us back on-line," said Charlene.

"Give me a second! Give me a second!" mumbled Justin. He hated messing up on the computer. It gave him a stomachache. Justin kept attacking the escape key.

"Hey, look!" shouted Charlene. She pointed to the screen.

"What's that?" asked Charlene.

Then the symbols changed into letters that read:

INVITATION TO DOOM!

CHAPTER 2
Great Minds Think Alike

Suddenly the screen went blank again and the modem made funny noises.

"What's happening?" asked Ms. Grace.

"We're cut off," said Justin.

Charlene shivered. "We're invited to doom."

"Doom," mumbled Chip. "I don't like the sound of that."

"What's the matter, invisible boy? Is it a little too scary for you?" said Keith.

"Keith, that's not the way you talk to someone in my library... or anywhere for that matter," said Ms. Grace.

Chip stuck out his tongue at Keith. Chip would get in trouble for doing that if the librarian saw him. But, of course, Ms. Grace couldn't see his tongue. That was the good news about being invisible. The teachers never saw when you stuck out your tongue. The bad news was that neither could Keith. Chip rolled his eyes up toward the ceiling. Sometimes being invisible was really tough!

"What are we going to do about this invitation to doom?" Charlene asked.

"Nothing," said Chip. "What can we do about it?"

"But we have to find out who sent this," said Charlene. "We're Invisible Inc. and we solve mysteries. It's our job!"

"Well, we know one thing," said Justin. "The person who sent that message knows how to use a computer."

The next day Ms. Grace printed out the live chat with U.B. Spooks. She gave it to Justin.

Justin read through the chat. "I can't believe it. Here was our chance to invite U.B. Spooks to our school. But none of our questions went through. U.B. Spooks doesn't even know we exist."

"We could ask him to our school through regular mail," said Ms. Grace. "I'll write to his publisher. But we'll have to raise the money to pay for his expenses and a fee."

"We can do that," said Charlene.

Justin felt cheerful again. Maybe U.B. Spooks could come to their school after all. Justin got busy at the computer. He was making a birthday card for his mom. He made a picture of a birthday cake. Then he used the mouse to color the cake purple, his mother's favorite color.

"That's beautiful," said Ms. Grace.

"Wait a minute! Wait a minute! Incoming idea!" shouted Charlene. Charlene always got excited about her own ideas. She jumped up and down.

"I've got one, too!" said Sandy. "We could raise money to get U.B. Spooks by selling computer greeting cards."

Charlene stared at her. "That was my idea!"

"Well, you know what we say on the computer. . . GMTA!" Justin typed the letters GMTA into the computer.

"What does that mean?" asked Chip. It was the first thing he had said in a long time.

"Great Minds Think Alike!" said Justin. He looked at Chip, who was working at the computer next to him. "Come on, buddy. You've got a computer. You know what the shorthand means."

"Yeah," said Chip. Chip did have a computer at home, but he wasn't as good on it as Justin.

"Making cards is an excellent idea," said Ms. Grace. "The PTA will buy cards. They always need invitations."

"We can make posters to advertise," said Sandy.

Justin sat at the computer while the other kids made suggestions.

"Let's make the letters bigger!"

"Let's make the letters fatter!"

"Let's make the words look like a heart."

"Pink and purple letters!"

"No! Red and blue letters!"

Justin was working so hard that he never noticed that Chip had walked away.

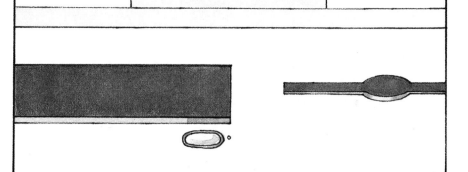

Justin finished the ad and sent it to the printer. But the library printer was backed up with other print jobs. And it was time for the class to go back to its room.

After recess the boys and girls went back to the library to get the copies of their poster. But instead of their posters, two pieces of paper were waiting for them. One read . . .

:—(:—B

The other paper read:

> *"BEWARE! Especially you, the girl who likes to boss people around —and you — the boy who is so good with comput-ers. You and your friend, the bossy girl, are invit-ed to . . . DOOM!"*

"Hey," said Sandy. "Do you think the boy who's so good with comput-ers could be Justin?"

"Wait a minute! Wait a minute!" Charlene wondered out loud. "Who's the bossy girl?"

Everybody stared at Charlene.

"The computer is writing about us!" said Justin.

He turned the first piece of paper around. "It's computer shorthand. Look at it sideways. **: - (** is a frowning face.

"I'm not exactly sure what **: - B** means, but **: - P** means 'I'm sticking my tongue out at you.' Someone is mad at us."

Nobody could see that the corners of Chip's mouth were turned down.

CHAPTER 3
Run-Away Candy

The orders for greeting cards came in fast. The PTA ordered invitations to the Book Fair. The new school secretary, Mrs. Skoops, bought thank-you cards.

"Maybe you could add 'Thank you for writing,'" she said.

"Thank you for writing what?" asked Charlene.

"Oh, uh . . . I get lots of mail," said Mrs. Skoops.

One of the kindergartners wanted invitations for her birthday party.

"I'm going to have the Puffy Players at my party," said Roshanna. "Can you draw pictures of them on the card?"

"Sure," said Charlene. "What do they look like?"

Roshanna shrugged. "I don't know."

Charlene's little brother, Stanley, turned to Roshanna. "I think you should get your cards at a store."

"Hey," said Charlene. "We're doing this for something important. We're going to ask U.B. Spooks to come to our school."

"Our teacher says that the kindergartners won't be invited," said Stanley. "The books are too scary. It's not fair."

"Life's not fair," Charlene said to her brother.

"Don't worry, Roshanna," Justin said. "We'll make great invitations. We'll go see what the Puffy Players look like!"

"We will?" said Charlene. "But we don't have time. We have a mystery to solve."

"It's more important to raise money to get U.B. Spooks!" Justin said.

After school, Chip got on his bicycle to go home. "Hey, Chip!" shouted Justin. "Aren't you coming with us?"

"No. I have to go home to walk Max," said Chip.

There was something odd in Chip's voice.

"We'll go with you," said Charlene. "We can pick up Max and then go to see the Puffy Players. Then we can try to find out who is trying to scare Invisible Inc."

She and Justin walked with Chip over to his house.

"You've been very quiet lately," said Charlene.

"You all have been so busy trying to get that author to come," said Chip.

"What do you mean, *you* all? Don't you mean, *we*?" asked Charlene. "We're Invisible Inc. We stick together."

"But I'm the only one who's invisible," Chip said to himself.

When they got to Chip's house, Max was glad to see them. The little brown tip of his tail waved back and forth. While Chip went upstairs, Justin looked at the papers around Chip's computer.

"What's taking Chip so long?" Charlene asked.

"Nothing," said Chip. "I've been down here for five minutes!"

Chip had changed into his invisible clothes.

"Well, let's get going," said Charlene. "We've got to go meet the Puffy Players." Justin put down the papers.

The Puffy Players had offices right above the little stationery store at the mall. Charlene, Justin, Chip, and Max walked up the stairs. They heard voices singing "Old MacDonald Had a Farm."

Max barked every time he heard
an "oink, oink."

Justin knocked on the door.
"Who's there?"

"Justin McCabe!" shouted Justin.

"Just in time!" said a voice
behind the door. Justin rolled his
eyes. He had heard that knock-
knock joke before.

The door was opened by a man in
a big puffy pig outfit. A woman was
in a cat outfit. Max growled at the
cat.

"Who's growling?" asked the pig.

"Quiet, Max," said Chip.

"Who said that?" asked a bunny.

"Me," said Chip.

The bunny stared into space. "Is one of you kids throwing your voice?"

"No," said Chip. "I'm invisible."

"Oh, we've heard about an invisible kid in town," said the pig.

Chip held on tight to Max's leash. He didn't really like being known as "that invisible kid."

"We're making invitations for a birthday party for a girl who hired you. Our customer wanted us to draw a picture of you," Charlene said.

"Sounds good," said the pig. "We usually get our ads printed down-stairs at the stationery store. But show us what you come up with. Maybe we'll use you."

Charlene and Justin were smiling as they left the shop. "That's great. Isn't it, Chip?" said Charlene. She looked around. Chip had disap-peared. "Chip?"

"Charlene," said Justin. "Something's wrong with Chip. I know it."

Justin saw Chip's knapsack by the curb. It was dented. Then he saw Max's leash. Justin poked above the knapsack.

"Chip?" asked Justin. "Are you sitting on your knapsack?"

"Go away," said Chip.

"What's wrong?" asked Justin.

Before Chip could answer, Charlene broke in. "What do they sell at a stationery store?" she asked.

"Stationery," said Chip. "Is this another dumb knock-knock joke . . . like the one the pig asked?"

"I thought the pig was cute," said Charlene. "But no. It's not a joke. I bet the store is losing money because people are starting to come to us for their cards. What if the stationery store owner is sending us scary notes so we'll quit?"

Justin scowled. "The scary messages started before we began making cards," he said.

"Maybe the first one was just a kid fooling around . . . and then the stationery store owner heard about our card business and sent the next scary message," said Charlene.

"Hmmm," said Justin. "It's true. Lots of people from the school go in there. Look, there goes Mrs. Skoops."

"I'm sure I've solved the crime," said Charlene. "We'll go into the stationery store and pretend to buy something. You stay invisible and sneak into the owner's office. Find out if his computer is hooked up to the one in the school library."

"You really are bossy sometimes," said Chip.

Chip hopped up. He gave Charlene his knapsack and snuck into the stationery store with Max.

Inside the store, Mrs. Skoops was buying paper. The store owner turned to Charlene and Justin. "May I help you kids?" he asked.

Mrs. Skoops screamed. She pointed toward the floor. A piece of candy was floating in the air.

Charlene whispered to Justin, "Max must have slipped out of his collar. We're in big trouble now!"

Suddenly the candy hopped up to the counter. The owner's eyes opened wide. "What was that?" he said.

"We'd better leave," said Charlene quickly. She and Justin ran out of the store. They met Chip and Max outside.

"That was close," said Chip. "Anyhow, I went into the owner's office. He didn't even have a computer."

Charlene sighed. "I guess we have to forget about him as a suspect. We're back at the beginning. I think we have to look closer at everybody at school."

"Maybe even closer than that," said Justin thoughtfully.

CHAPTER 4
Not a Freak—a Friend!

Chip sat down at his usual place during computer time. He was surprised to find a message for him:

Chip. I know your secret.
But **: - X**.

The message was signed GonzoJust. Chip rubbed his eyes. He tried very hard to remember how to read the symbol.

: - X was a face with its lips closed. It was the sign for keeping a secret. Justin was saying that he wouldn't tattle.

At recess, Chip met Justin near their favorite tree.

"How did you know it was me?" Chip asked into Justin's good ear.

"You've been acting funny all
week," said Justin. "When I was at
your house, I was looking at the
papers around your computer.
There was a mistake. On your paper
it said **: - B** for sticking out your
tongue instead of **: - P**—just like on
the paper I found at school. Why did
you want to stick out your tongue?"

"You told the author to come to

school to meet the invisible kid," said Chip. "It made me feel like a freak . . . not a friend. No one can ever see how I feel, so I used the computer to show it."

Justin put his hand on Chip's shoulder. "I'm sorry," he said. "I guess I didn't think. I got used to your being invisible. I didn't think you minded."

"Don't you mind sometimes that you have to wear a phonic ear and that you have trouble hearing?" Chip asked.

"Yeah," said Justin.

"Well, it's not always fun to be invisible either," said Chip. He patted Justin on the shoulder. All of a sudden they saw Charlene running toward them.

"Justin! Chip! Come quick!"

shouted Charlene. "I just went into
the library to pick up the invitations
we made for Roshanna's birthday
party. They're ruined! Look at this."
Charlene showed them the cards.

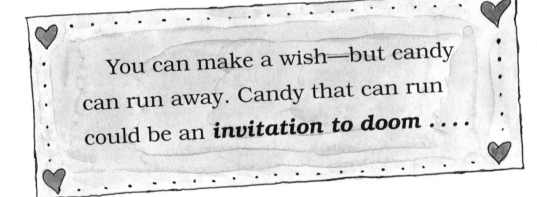

You can make a wish—but candy
can run away. Candy that can run
could be an *invitation to doom* . . . .

"That stuff about invitation to
doom doesn't belong on a birthday
invitation for little kids!" Charlene
said. "We've got to catch the person

who's been sending these terrible messages!"

"We have caught the person," said Justin. "Chip, I think you'd better tell her."

"Tell her what?" said Chip. "I didn't do anything to Roshanna's invitations."

"What about the PTA Book Fair announcements? And all the other *invitations to doom* that came out of the printer?" asked Justin.

"That wasn't me! I just sent the one note . . . sticking my tongue out at everybody. I was mad because

nobody can ever really see me frown or stick out my tongue."

"Didn't you write all that invitation to doom stuff?" asked Justin.

"Of course not. Who do you think I am, U.B. Spooks?" asked Chip.

CHAPTER 5
Too Weird to Be True

Chip took one of Roshanna's birthday invitations and read it again. "'Candy that can run by itself.' It sounds like Max in the stationery store."

"It does!" said Charlene. "But if you didn't write it, who did?"

"Spooks!" said Justin.

"Where?" said Charlene. "Who are you trying to scare?"

"Spooks! Right here! Right in our school!" said Justin mysteriously. "Let's go to the library."

"U.B. Spooks likes the sound of 'ooo,'" said Justin. "Who else do we know who has a name with 'ooo' in it?"

"Mrs. Skoops?" asked Charlene. "But she's so nice."

"Nice and spooky," said Justin.
"SKOOPS spelled backward is
SPOOKS!"

Justin asked Ms. Grace if he
could have a copy of U.B. Spooks'
Slime on the Playground. "I'm going
to get it autographed."

Ms. Grace looked very confused.

Justin, Chip, and Charlene took the book to the office. Mrs. Skoops looked up from her work. "Hi, kids," she said. "What can I do for you?"

"Can you autograph this book for me?" said Justin.

Mrs. Skoops put her hand over her mouth. She looked embarrassed. "How did you know?"

"We're Invisible Inc. We know everything," bragged Charlene. "We even know you're next book is *Invitation to Doom*! And we know that one of your characters is like me and one of your characters is like Justin."

"How did you know that?" Mrs. Skoops asked.

"We keep getting your printouts in the library," said Chip.

"I wondered what happened to them," said Mrs. Skoops. "If I don't connect my computer the right way in the morning, my copies go all over the place! I've been searching high and low for the new chapter that I've been writing during my break."

"Well, it went to the library," said Justin. "And it kept getting into our invitations. We were raising money to bring you to the school and you're already here."

"I know," said Mrs. Skoops. "But I couldn't tell you until I finished my new book. I like my characters to seem real. So I study real kids to find out what they do. That's why I took this job."

"Real kids solve mysteries," said Chip.

"And you're very good at it," said Mrs. Skoops.

"Are you going to put an invisible boy in your next story?" asked Charlene.

Mrs. Skoops smiled. "I don't know," she said. "It's almost too unusual to be true. Would anyone believe it?"

"We would," said Charlene and Justin together. They put their arms around Chip.